MOMS CAN'T GET SICK!
Written by Sarah Barstow ◆ Illustrations by Mandy K.J. Brown

This book is dedicated to all of the moms out there who are able to push past their own sickness to care for those they love so dearly. And, of course, to Nemi & Zinny, who have shown me just how deep my capacity to love is.

-S.B.

Moms Can't Get Sick by Sarah Barstow
Illustrated by Mandy K.J. Brown
1st Edition

Summary: Mom isn't feeling well. But getting sick isn't always an option when you have little (and big) ones to care for. Good thing Moms are experts at putting other peoples needs before their own.

ISBN 978-0-578-56917-8

1. Parenting Humor 2. Mother & Child 3. Baby & Toddler Parenting Challenges
4. Humor 5. Mothers

Precious Zinny
was just turning one.
The cutest lil baby under the sun.
Steady on his feet, and walking all around.
He slept through the night and made not a sound.

Then, one
winter's night he
was sounding quite sick,
so Mama ran to him quick, quick, quick.
His mouth opened wide & much to her surprise,
vomit sprayed her face & dripped down her eyes.

But that's okay Mama.
No need to despair.
Getting sick yourself just wouldn't be fair.
But oh no, there it is: the cough and the chills.
Mama, poor Mama, is indeed very ill.

But who has time
to get sick with a baby?
A day spent puking isn't possible. That's crazy!
You puke while he's napping. What else can you do?
You're just under the weather. You can't have the flu.

Wash those hands,

scrub them, & wash them some more.

Disinfect the countertops and bleach the floor.

Build up those immunities & build them up quick.

Let's be real, MOMS CAN'T GET SICK!

Little Zinny was just turning two,
He loved soccer and dump trucks & trips to the zoo.
He was happy and silly and laughed quite a lot.
Everyone agreed he was a super great tot.

Then, one winter's night
he was feeling quite bad.
He wanted his Mama, he wouldn't take Dad.
When Mama rushed to him, he coughed in her face,
& his gross toddler germs went all over the place.

Will this affect Mama?
        Certainly Not!
She keeps wiping boogies of lovely green snot.
She snuggles him, sings songs and sleeps in his bed,
while the germs she's absorbing quickly fill her with dread.

Hang in there Mama. You don't dare get sick.
Better bust out the tinctures lickety split.
No need to worry, you won't get sick at all.
Uh oh, is that big brother puking down the hall?

Two sick kids means
the germs have been doubled.
Time to enclose yourself in an airtight bubble?
Maybe it's time to run away. Run away quick!
Because now, dear lord, Dad's also sick.

Get to it Mama:

take temperatures, change sheets.

Make the rounds with the sickies, while acting upbeat.

Try to take care of yourself, can more sleep be the trick?

Let's be real, MOMS CAN'T GET SICK!

Written by Sarah Barstow

Sarah always says that parenting is the "Best. Hardest thing you'll ever do!" Having a sense of humor definitely helps! When she's not navigating the waters of raising a toddler and a teenager at the same time, you can find her curled up with a book, hiking or working in her boutique,The Rave'N Image. This book fulfills Sarah's childhood dream of becoming an author. Although, her 8 year old self couldn't have known that it would take her nearly 4 decades to finally be published. And she definitely wouldn't have guessed that the book would involve quite so much puke.

You can contact Sarah at theravenimage@yahoo.com

Illustrations by Mandy K.J. Brown

Mandy K. J. Brown is a multifaceted artist; often mystified, yet down to earth and curiously present. This isn't surprising, as she was born and raised in the eclectic town of Moab Utah. In love with life, she enjoys bringing dreams to reality through her artistic crafts. She paints murals, oracle cards, portraits and custom art. Creating illustrations for self published authors comes naturally to her, as she sees it as helping to create family heirlooms.

You can contact Mandy at mandykjbrown@gmail.com